Ruth Martin

Moon Dreams

illustrated by Olivier Latyk

To Doreen and Steve
O. L.

For Mum, who always watches over me, and for my new baby, Tabitha
R. M.

First published in the U.K. in 2010 as *Where on Earth Is the Moon?*

First U.S. edition 2010

Library of Congress Cataloging-in-Publication Data is available.
Library of Congress Catalog Card Number pending.
ISBN 978-0-7636-5012-4

10 11 12 13 14 15 16 TLF 10 9 8 7 6 5 4 3 2 1

Printed in Dongguan, Guangdong, China.
This book was typeset in Litterbox ICG.
The illustrations were created digitally.

Edited by Emma Goldhawk
Designed by Leonard Le Rolland

TEMPLAR BOOKS

an imprint of Candlewick Press
99 Dover Street
Somerville, Massachusetts 02144
www.candlewick.com

Ruth Martin

Moon Dreams

illustrated by Olivier Latyk

templar books
an imprint of Candlewick Press

Luna had always loved the Moon.

On the night she was born, a full Moon had filled the sky—
brighter, rounder, and bigger than ever before. And as she grew,
Luna always felt sure that the Moon watched over her
from the dark night sky.

Every night Luna would gaze at the Moon
from her bedroom window before she fell asleep.

The Moon was so quiet and so pretty in the sky that it made her
feel calm and peaceful as she slipped off to sleep.

Luna often dreamed of the Moon: crescent moons, half moons, and full moons— even of walking on the Moon!

But every morning when she woke up,
the Moon had always vanished from the sky.

Where does the Moon go all day?

Luna wondered.

She was determined to find out.

So, as the Sun set that evening . . .

Luna decided she would stay
awake all night . . .

to see where the Moon went . . .

when it disappeared
each morning.

From her bedroom that night, Luna listened
to the ocean waves. Perhaps the Moon slips softly
into the ocean during the day, she thought.

WhoOsh . . . wash, whoOsh . . . wash went the waves.
Luna tried hard to stay awake,
but soon she fell into a dreamy sleep. . . .

Luna woke up remembering a lovely dream of the ocean.
She had seen a giant fish that glowed like the Moon,
but the Moon itself wasn't hiding under the sea.

When nighttime came again,
Luna looked out at the Moon
beyond the distant mountains.

Maybe the Moon rolls far, far away,
down behind the mountains, she thought.

Ch-ch, ch-ch, chirped the crickets.
Twit-twoo, hooted the owl.
Though Luna tried not to,
she soon felt herself falling
into a dreamy sleep. . . .

The next morning, Luna remembered dreaming of beautiful mountains and a frozen lake shaped just like the Moon, but the Moon wasn't there among the hills and valleys.

It rained and stormed all day long, and as bedtime drew near, Luna could barely see the Moon behind the raging black clouds.

Perhaps, she pondered, the Moon
just hides behind the clouds all day.
Once again, Luna tried as hard as
she could to stay awake all night.

But drip, drop, drippy-drop, poured the rain, and
soon Luna's eyes were closing as she drifted
off again into a dreamy sleep. . . .

When Luna woke up the next morning, the storm
had passed. She knew she'd dreamed of the Sun
shining high in the sky behind the clouds,
but the Moon had not been there.

That evening as Luna climbed into bed,
she still couldn't imagine where
the Moon went each day.

Could there be a place, beyond the ocean, higher than the mountains,
and far, far above the clouds where the Moon goes every morning?
Luna wondered as she fell into a dreamy sleep.

Luna's dream took her into space. She saw all the planets and stars. And there, at last, was the Moon—brighter, rounder, and bigger than ever before.

"Where **do** you go in the daytime?" Luna asked the Moon.

"I'm always here in space, watching over you," the Moon replied.

"But you can only see me at night, when the sky is dark."

Luna woke up happily the next morning, remembering that she'd finally found the Moon in her dreams.

Luna knew now that the Moon
was always there, far away in space,
watching over her—and every night
at bedtime she would see it,
shining in the dark sky.